MORE SPECIAL OFFERS
FOR MR MEN AND LITTLE MISS

In every Mr Men and Little Miss book like this one, <u>and now</u> in the Mr Men sticker and activity books, you will find a special token. Collect six tokens and we will send you a gift of your choice

Choose either a <u>Mr Men</u> <u>or</u> <u>Little Miss</u> poster, **or** a Mr Men or Little Miss **double sided** full colour bedroom door hanger.

Return this page **with six tokens per gift required** to:
Marketing Dept., MM / LM, World International Ltd.,
PO Box 7, Manchester, M19 2HD

Your name:_____ Age: _____

Address: _____

_____

_____Postcode: _____

Parent / Guardian Name (Please Print)_____

Please tape a 20p coin to your request to cover part post and package cost

I enclose <u>six</u> tokens per gift, and 20p please send me:-

<u>Posters:-</u>   Mr Men Poster   ☐   Little Miss Poster   ☐
<u>Door Hangers</u> - Mr Nosey / Muddle   ☐   Mr Greedy / Lazy   ☐
              Mr Tickle / Grumpy   ☐   Mr Slow / Busy   ☐
              Mr Messy / Quiet   ☐   Mr Perfect / Forgetful ☐
              L Miss Fun / Late   ☐   L Miss Helpful / Tidy ☐
              L Miss Busy / Brainy ☐   L Miss Star / Fun   ☐

Please Tick Appropriate Box

20p

Stick 20p here please

We may occasionally wish to advise you of other Mr Men gifts.
If you would rather we didn't please tick this box   ☐

— 100 mm —

ENTRANCE FEE
3 SAUSAGES

250 mm

MR. GREEDY

Collect six of these tokens
You will find one inside every
Mr Men and Little Miss book
which has this special offer.

1
TOKEN

Offer open to residents of UK, Channel Isles and Ireland only

Mr Men and Little Miss Library Presentation Boxes

In response to the many thousands of requests for the above, we are delighted to advise that these are now available direct from ourselves,
for only **£4.99 (inc VAT) plus 50p p&p.**
The full colour boxes accommodate each complete library. They have an integral carrying handle as well as a neat stay closed fastener.
Please do not send cash in the post. Cheques should be made payable to **World International Ltd. for the sum of £5.49 (inc p&p) per box.**

Please note books are not included.

Please return this page with your cheque, stating below which presentation box you would like, to:-
**Mr Men Office, World International
PO Box 7, Manchester, M19 2HD**

Your name:_____

Address: _____

_____

_____Postcode: _____

Name of Parent/Guardian (please print):_____

Signature:_____

I enclose a cheque for £_____ made payable to World International Ltd.,

Please send me a Mr Men Presentation Box ☐

            Little Miss Presentation Box ☐   (please tick or write in quantity)
and allow 28 days for delivery

Thank you

Offer applies to UK, Eire & Channel Isles only

little Miss Fun

by Roger Hargreaves

WORLD INTERNATIONAL

Little Miss Fun was as happy
as a lark.

Except when she is organising a party.

And then …

She is even happier than a lark.

Little Miss Fun simply adores parties

And she likes to invite lots and lots
of people to her parties.

The other Sunday, there were a lot of people making their way to Little Miss Fun's house.

Mr Funny was making funny faces.
Mr Lazy was yawning.
Mr Clumsy was falling over.

And Mr Tall was walking in very small steps ...
So he would not arrive too early!

Mr Forgetful was not with them.
He was at home. Reading a book.
He'd forgotten all about Little Miss Fun's party!

"Never mind,"
laughed Little Miss Fun.
"We can start the party without him!"

She put a record on the record-player.

The record went round and round,
and the music played.

Little Miss Fun asked
Mr Clumsy to dance with her.

And he accepted.

Unfortunately, he stood on her right foot.

"Never mind," she laughed.

Then she ran off to ask Mr Lazy to dance.

Unfortunately, when he put his head on
her shoulder, he fell asleep.

And almost flattened her!

"Never mind!" she laughed.

In less than an hour,
Little Miss Fun had made everybody dance:

… the Rumba and the Samba,

… the Rock-and-Roll and the Twist,

… the Charleston and the Cha-Cha-Cha.

Then she led everybody out into the garden.

And they danced all around the house.

All the flowers in the garden were trampled.

"Never mind!"
said Little Miss Fun.
"Let's go back indoors."

"Let's play Simon Says … ,"
she cried.

"Simon Says … put your feet in the air!"

There was a loud CRASH!

As Mr Tall's foot smashed through the window pane and shattered it!

"Never mind,"
laughed Little Miss Fun.

And she jumped on to the table
so she could pretend to be a clown
and make her friends laugh.

But nobody laughed.

No wonder!

Everybody was exhausted.

They had all fallen asleep.

"Never mind!" laughed
Little Miss Fun.

And she carried on pretending to be a clown.

Who was she doing it for,
now that everybody was asleep?

Well, she was doing it for a little bird
who had flown in through the broken window.

But there's someone else she is doing it for,
isn't there?